TINY
T. REX

AND THE IMPOSSIBLE HUG

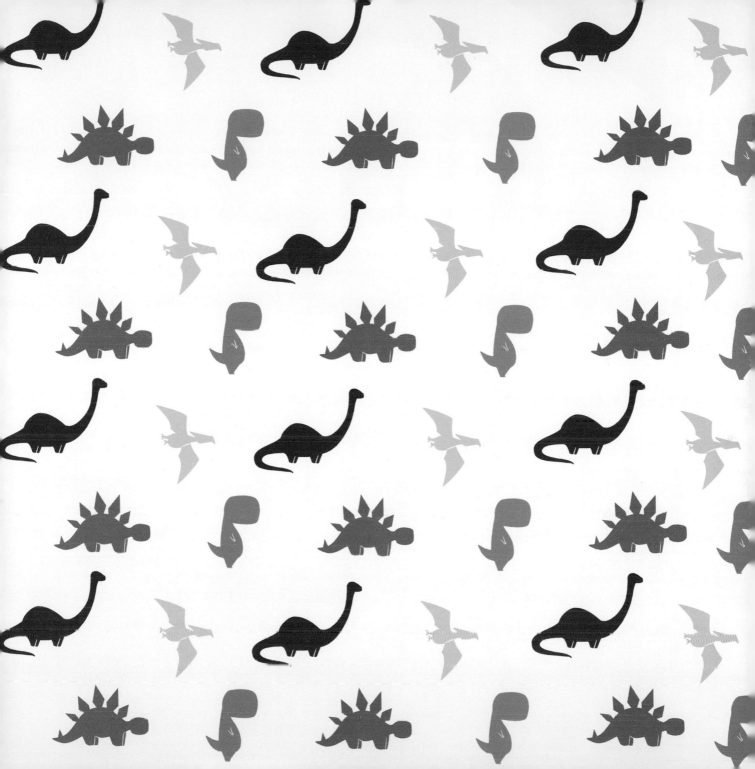

Hello, Pointy! Are you OK?

No, today I feel sad. I do not want to play.

TINY T. REX

SCHOLASTIC INC.

AND THE IMPOSSIBLE HUG

by Jonathan Stutzman   illustrated by Jay Fleck

HOW TO MAKE
A FRIEND
FEEL BETTER

· CAKE
· SMILES
· HUGS
· TACOS
· JOKES

I have tiny arms.

It is very difficult to hug with tiny arms.

Each day I am growing taller,
but my arms are still tiny.

Hugging almost seems impossible
for a Rex as tiny as me,
but I will try anyway.
Pointy needs me.

Where is my father?
I will ask him for advice.

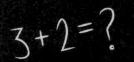

$3 + 2 = ?$ $7 + 3 = ?$ $5 + 3 = ?$

Rexes are thinkers, not huggers.
Perhaps instead of hugs, mathematics
might be the answer to your problem?

$$x + y$$
$$x + y + z$$

$$\underline{happiness} = 8x + 3y + 2z$$

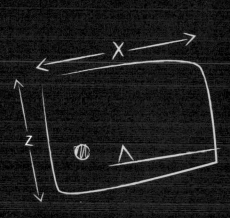

Pointy does not like math.

Math will only make Pointy feel worse.

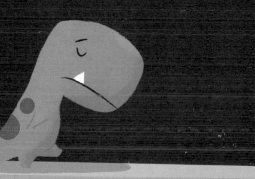

HELLO, AUNTIE JUNIP!

I have a problem.
I must learn how to hug, but my arms
are too tiny.

I have found that balance is the key to every problem. Balance and freshly squeezed cucumber juice.

That is disgusting. I will ask my mother for help instead.

I have fallen and now I am lost.

I do not think I will find my
mother in here.

It's okay if you can't hug, Tiny. You are good at many other things. You are kind and creative and braver than most. You are tiny, but your heart is big!

I cannot hug with my heart, Mother.
I must learn to hug with my arms.

HELLO, SISTER!
HELLO, BROTHER!

Please help me.
Hugging is very difficult.

We'd love to help, Tiny!

To do the impossible you must plan and practice.

Practice,

practice,

practice.

Thank you, Trixie and Rawrie. That is good advice.

I will plan my strategy.

I will get stronger.

I will practice very hard.
I will practice my hugs on everything!

I will not practice on that anymore.

I am almost ready. I will practice
one more time. When I am done,
I will find my friend.

This tree is very big, like Pointy.

I will hug it.

This is not a tree.
I have made a mistake.

Please help.

From up here, everything looks tiny, like me.
I could hug anything I wanted.

I am here to make you feel better!
I have practiced very hard and hugged
many things.

My arms are still tiny and my hugs are still tiny, but I will do my very best because you are my very best friend.

Thank you, Tiny.

That was the biggest hug ever.

For Fox, my favorite one to hug – J. S.
To anyone that needs a hug – J. F.

ISBN 978-1-338-65204-8

12 11 10 9   21 22 23 24 25

Printed in the U.S.A.   40

First Scholastic printing, January 2020

Design by Jennifer Tolo Pierce

Typeset in Intelo and Brandon Printed

The illustrations in this book were rendered in pencil and colored digitally.

JONATHAN STUTZMAN is an award-winning filmmaker
and writer of books for children. His short films have screened
around the world and on television, and he is a contributing
writer to the bestselling collection *The Tiny Book of Tiny Stories*.
Despite his association with tiny things, he is actually rather tall.
Jonathan loves reading, making up stories, and being silly. He
lives in the wilds of Lancaster, Pennsylvania, with his wife and
French bulldog, and he is a staunch believer in impossible things
and the power of hugs.

JAY FLECK is an Illinois-based designer and illustrator.
Inspired by memories from childhood as well as his two young
children, his art has been featured everywhere from the Gap to
Papyrus to Threadless. He lives with his family south of Chicago,
and spends his spare time running and reading (but not at the
same time).